Table of contents

Amazing Ducks

Birds that live in and near the water are called **waterfowl**. Ducks belong in the waterfowl family.

Ducks have webbed feet that help them swim fast.

Ducks have two layers of feathers. The outer layer is waterproof. The inner layer of soft, fluffy feathers, called **down**, keeps the duck warm.

A male duck is called a drake. A female duck is called a duck.

Drake

Did you know that drakes don't quack? Only the female duck does!

Work! Work! Work!

Ducks live in the **wild** or on a farm. In the wild, ducks care for themselves. On a farm, they need some help.

Farmers keep the ducks on the farm safe, healthy, and happy.

Ducks need many of the same things that you do. First, they need a shelter to protect them during the cold winters or the very warm summers.

A Duck Farmer's List

☑ *Fresh water for my ducks to drink and play in*

☑ *Healthy food for my ducks to eat*

☑ *Space for my ducks to explore*

☑ *A clean place for my ducks to live*

It's a Duck's Life

Ducks spend their time eating, napping, and swimming.

Ducks live in a pasture, in a fenced yard, or on a pond. At night, they nest in a large shelter such as a shed or barn.

Ducks eat many foods, including plants, worms, and insects. They also eat grains such as corn and wheat along with **grit**.

Grit consists of pebbles that help grind up the duck's food in its stomach.

Baby Ducks

The mother duck builds her nest out of grass or straw. For almost 28 days, the mother duck sits on her eggs to keep them warm.

Farm ducks lay eggs all year round.

Depending on the breed, a duck can lay between 80 and 300 eggs in a single year!

When the baby duck, called a duckling, is ready to **hatch**, it will break out of the egg.

In just one year, the duckling grows up and lays eggs of her own.

Duck Helpers

Ducks help people in many ways. Ducks lay lots of eggs for us to eat. Ducks are also raised for meat.

Pillows, blankets, and coats made from duck feathers, called down, keep people warm and cozy.

Down

People love ducks. We like to feed them and watch them splash and play.

Glossary

down (DOUN): a layer of soft, fluffy feathers

grit (GRIT): small rocks birds swallow to help digest their food

hatch (HACH): to break out of an egg

waterfowl (waw-TER-foul): a bird that lives near rivers, lakes, or oceans

wild (WILDE): living in nature, without human help

Index

Websites to Visit

www.kiddyhouse.com/Farm/ducks.html

www.kidskonnect.com/subject-index/13-animals/438-ducks.html

www.abc.net.au/creaturefeatures/facts/ducks.htm

About the Author

Kyla Steinkraus lives in Tampa, FL with her family. Kyla and her four-year-old son like to feed the wild ducks at the park.